To:

From:

To my daughter Tess, who was born on
Christmas Eve, and who has always known her own mind
— L.B.

To Tara and my lovely friends
Myriam and Emily for their ideas and support
— G.G.

Text copyright © 2015 by Linda Bailey
Illustrations copyright © 2015 by Geneviève Godbout

Tundra Books, a division of Random House of Canada Limited, a
Penguin Random House Company

Library and Archives Canada Cataloguing in Publication

Bailey, Linda, 1948- author
        When Santa was a baby / by Linda Bailey ; illustrated
by Geneviève Godbout.

Available in print and in electronic formats.
ISBN 978-1-77049-556-2 (bound).—ISBN 978-1-77049-558-6
(epub)

        I. Godbout, Geneviève, 1985-, illustrator II. Title.

PS8553.A3644W396 2015   jC813'.54   C2014-906428-4
                                               C2014-906429-2

Published simultaneously in the United States of America by Tundra
Books of Northern New York, a division of Random House of Canada
Limited, a Penguin Random House Company

Library of Congress Control Number: 2014951820

Edited by Tara Walker
Designed by Terri Nimmo
The artwork in this book was rendered in pastels and colored pencils.
The text was set in Filosofia.

Printed and bound in China

Tundra Books,
a division of Random House of Canada Limited,
a Penguin Random House Company
www.penguinrandomhouse.ca

1 2 3 4 5   19 18 17 16 15

WHEN SANTA WAS A BABY

Written by LINDA BAILEY

Illustrated by GENEVIÈVE GODBOUT

TUNDRA BOOKS

When Santa was a baby, he was soft and round and cuddly,
and his parents thought he was wonderful.

"Look at those dimples," said his dad. "How merry!"

"And his dear little nose," said his mom. "Like a cherry!"

"Kitchy-kitchy goo!" they said together and waited for Santa
to make a baby sound. A sweet little gurgle. A gentle coo.

HO, HO!"

boomed baby Santa in a voice that rattled the windows.

"Oh my!" said his parents, leaping back. "What was *that*?"

Little Santa smiled his first smile. His parents were thrilled.

"He doesn't have the *usual* baby voice," said his dad.

"But it's good and strong, isn't it?"

"It's special," said his mom. "Just like him."

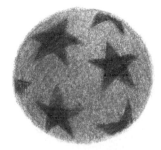

The years went by, and Santa grew older. He began to learn his colors. Right from the start, he liked red best.

"What about these dandy blue pajamas from Aunt Mabel?" said his mom.

Santa shook his head. "Want red!"

"Of course you do," said his dad.

"But blue is nice too."

"Want *red*!" said little Santa.

His parents put the blue pajamas in a drawer.

"Maybe he'll be a firefighter," said his mom.

*O*n his next birthday, Santa got a beautiful red fire truck
from his mom and dad. He got a rocking horse from
Grandma, a puzzle from Uncle Ned and a pair of yellow
pajamas from Aunt Mabel.

What a lovely time Santa had opening his presents!
He had an even *lovelier* time wrapping them up again
and putting them in a sack.

"What's he doing?" asked his mom.

"Beats me," said his dad.

They watched in amazement as Santa rode down
the street, giving away his presents to all the boys and girls.
"Did you ever see anything like it?" said Santa's mom.
His dad shook his head. "What a generous child!"

On his *next* birthday, Santa asked for a horse.

Well, it wasn't *exactly* a horse. He said it was *like* a horse, except it had horns and could pull a flying sled. His parents didn't understand, so they asked him to draw it.

"Do you think it's a unicorn?" said Santa's dad, scratching his head.

"A unicorn!" said his mom. "Now where are we supposed to get one of those?"

They got him a hamster instead.

It was a female hamster, and soon it had eight babies. When they grew big enough, Santa harnessed them with ribbons to a matchbox. He put tiny presents in the matchbox and trained the hamsters to pull it around the house.

"Listen!" said his mom. "He's calling them by name."

"Dasher," said Santa, "and Dancer and Comet . . . and, um, Blixen. No, Vixen!"

"Extraordinary!" said Santa's dad.

"He's so creative," said his mom.

Santa was an unusual child in many ways.

For one thing, he didn't like warm weather.
When the other children were running
around in the hot summer sun, little Santa
stayed inside, waiting for the fridge
door to open.

"We can't keep it open *all* the time," said his mom. "Think of the electric bills."

"You're right," sighed his dad, "but it makes him so happy."

*S*anta also had an odd interest in chimneys.

"What do you suppose he's looking at?" asked his dad.

"His clothes are all covered in ashes and soot."

"We can wash them," said his mom.

"Isn't it great that he's so curious?"

"Maybe he'll be a scientist," said his dad.

Santa's best friend lived right next door.

His name was Eldred. Eldred was smaller than Santa, but in other ways they were very much alike. They both enjoyed making things — especially toys. And Eldred loved *green* almost as much as Santa loved red!

"What a jolly pair!" said Santa's mom.

"So nice to have a friend!" said Santa's dad.

As Santa got older, it became clear he'd inherited the family good looks.

"Goodness," said Santa's mom. "Just look at your bellies. They match!"

"Like two bowls full of jelly," said Santa's dad. "Ha, ha, ha."

"Tee, hee, hee," said Santa's mom.

"HO, HO, HO!"

boomed Santa.

When Santa became a teenager, he continued
to be unusual. He knew his own mind.
He didn't always fit in with the crowd.
But his parents thought he was wonderful.

As for the rest of the story . . .
well, you can probably guess.
Santa followed his childhood dreams.

He moved to the North Pole, where it's very cold. He built a toy-making workshop and brought in a crew of elves to help. He got a big, beautiful sleigh and trained eight reindeer to pull it.

And once a year, he travels around the world, climbing down chimneys to leave gifts for boys and girls.

His parents are so proud they could burst! Every Christmas Eve, they listen for his sleigh bells. They wave and blow kisses as Santa dips low over their house.

"It's what we always *thought* he'd do," says his mom.

"We *knew* it all the time!" says his dad.

And what do you think Santa says to that?